SANTA'S
HIGH-TECH
CHRISTMAS

MIKE DUMBLETON AND ANGELA PERRINI

Long before each Christmas Day,
Santa works hard on his sleigh.

He carefully uses touch-up paint
on every scratch, however faint.

And with a love of high-tech gear,
he makes improvements every year.

This year, as parcels fill his sleigh,
he checks them off the modern way.

He scans the presents, really fast,
not writing names as in the past.

And all the lists that Santa had are now on his new techno-pad.

Santa's sleigh is weatherproof,
with a fancy flip-top roof.

And Santa finds it quite a treat
in his soft reclining seat.

He makes good time in the dark,
in places where there's room to park.

But crowded cities are a worry,
and Santa knows he has to hurry.

He parks the sleigh and fills his sack,
then uses his new ...

rocket-pack!

Things were going just as planned

until his pad slipped from his hand.

'What was that?' a young girl said,
now wide awake and out of bed.

Santa slowly turned around
and made a desperate sighing sound.

'The screen's gone blank! It won't come on.
My list of names and gifts is gone.'

The young girl spoke out eagerly,
'I'm Jasmin, Santa. Let me see.'
With skill and speed she tapped and scrolled,
making Santa feel quite old.

'I've got it working,' Jasmin said,
still puzzled by a list she'd read.

'If things go wrong when you're alone,
just tap my name to call my phone.'

'You're amazing!' Santa said.
Then he smiled and shook his head.
'This present hardly seems enough
after all that clever stuff.'

Jasmin found it hard to sleep,
expecting that her phone would beep.

And late that night, she had a call,
which came as no surprise at all.

Santa sounded quite distressed.
'I've got a problem,' he confessed.

'I scanned the presents but I missed
a gift for one girl on my list.'

'I thought so,' Jasmin quietly said.
'So she can have my gift instead.

Secretly, I gave it back.

It's in ...

your pocket, not your sack.'
Santa gave a heartfelt sigh,
so Jasmin added, in reply ...

'This year's present
was meeting you.

But next year, Santa ...

bring me two!'